# Bee Calm

## The Buzz on Yoga

by Frank J. Sileo, PhD

illustrated by Claire Keay

MAGINATION PRESS · WASHINGTON, DC

American Psychological Association

*To my cousin Debbie. May you always find peace in your heart and life*—FJS

*For Elis and John, with love*—CK

American Psychological Association
750 First Street NE
Washington, DC 20002

Magination Press is a registered trademark of the American Psychological Association. Order books here: maginationpress.org, or call 1-800-374-2721.

Book design by Susan K. White
Printed by Worzalla, Stevens Point, WI

**Library of Congress Cataloging-in-Publication Data**
*Names:* Sileo, Frank J., 1967– author | Keay, Claire, illustrator.
*Title:* Bee calm : the buzz on yoga / by Frank J. Sileo, PhD ; illustrated by Claire Keay.
*Description:* Washington, DC : Magination Press, [2019] | "American Psychological Association."
*Summary:* Illustrations and rhyming text tell of Bentley the bee who, while buzzing around the garden, sees his friends in strange positions and learns why each practices yoga. Includes note for parents.
*Identifiers:* LCCN 2018017576| ISBN 9781433829574 (hardcover) | ISBN 1433829576 (hardcover)
*Subjects:* | CYAC: Stories in rhyme. | Yoga—Fiction. | Bees—Fiction.
*Classification:* LCC PZ8.3.S58254 Bec 2019 | DDC [E]—dc23 LC record available at
https://lccn.loc.gov/2018017576

Manufactured in the United States of America
10 9 8 7 6 5 4 3 2 1

Bentley Bee lives in a hive
in a beautiful place,
with colorful flowers
and open space.

He loves to fly around and visit friends, too.
From up above, he has a bee's-eye view!

One day it was warm, with bright sunlight.
The perfect day to go for a flight!

First, Bentley flew to the top of the hill.
There was Pat Possum, standing still.

"Pat, why are you standing there, looking up at the sky?"
"I'm doing yoga. This is Mountain pose. Give it a try!"

"No thanks," said Bentley. "Yoga looks strange to me. Anyway, I've got other friends to go see."

Next Bentley went to visit his pal Bernie Bunny.
He was standing in a way that looked kind of funny.

Bernie was squatting like he was in a chair.
But there was nothing underneath him. He was sitting on air!

"I'm doing yoga," said Bernie. "This is called Chair pose.
I balance my body and breathe through my nose."

Bentley flew to the evergreen tree and saw Jane Blue Jay.
*Bee*-wildered he asked, "Why are you standing that way?"

"This is a yoga pose called Airplane. It helps me concentrate," said Jane.

Then something caught Bentley's eye. He couldn't help but stare.
Freddy Fox was in the grass with his tail in the air!

Bentley was curious. "What is this pose called, Freddy?"
"Downward Dog!" he replied as he tried to be steady.

Bentley flew on. He saw Abby Ant on a rose.
She was also in an unusual pose.

"That pose looks fun. Could you teach it to me?"
"Of course!" said Abby. "This pose is called Tree."

"Put your foot below your knee," Abby said.

"Place your hands by your chest or over your head."

Bentley tried to balance his body. He began to wiggle.
"I'm a tree!" he said, and he started to giggle.

"I like this pose," said Bentley. "But what's all the buzz? What is yoga? I'm still not sure what it does."

"Yoga exercises the body and mind.
It helps me focus, feel calm, and unwind."

"The practice of yoga began a long time ago.
Give it a try. Be patient and go slow.

Yoga should feel good so don't push or strain.
Stop what you're doing if you feel any pain."

Bentley tried other poses. He felt unsure.
He kept an open mind and tried some more.

He learned Warrior,

Child,

and Cobra pose too.

The more he practiced, the more he could do.

Soon Bentley was doing yoga alone,

with friends,

whenever he could.

Although it could be tricky, it made him feel good.

Now, once a day, Bentley takes a yoga break.
Afterward he feels peaceful, refreshed, and awake.

So practice like Bentley. Find a quiet place. Do a pose. Take a deep breath and see how it goes.

You've learned the buzz on yoga. Your practice has begun.
Be gentle with yourself. Remember to have fun!

# Note to Parents and Caregivers
## by Allison Morgan, MA, OTR, E-RYT

Exploring yoga with your child is a wonderful way to connect and exercise together. Although the practice of yoga began thousands of years ago, the need for its benefits has never been greater. In our fast-paced, busy lives, we don't always realize how our *go, go, go* lifestyle hinders our general health and hurts our most precious relationships. We tend to survive in a stressed mode of being, just to keep up with the pace. Unfortunately, this is what we end up modeling for our children. It is no wonder that we have rising rates of anxiety and chronic stress amongst even our youngest children.

Yoga teaches us how to stop, breathe, and notice how we feel in the moment. This allows us to respond to our daily situations and interactions with greater awareness. When we bring this awareness to our life, we have the opportunity to acknowledge our innate desire to be happy, joyful, and peaceful. These traits are so important, but often neglected. Research has shown that our state of mind, our body, and our breath have a tremendous effect on our sense of happiness. The practice of yoga balances our nervous system so we can become calm, focused, and resilient. Imagine teaching these skills to your child through playful poses combined with conscious breathing and focused attention.

### How to Use This Book
Reading about Bentley Bee and his friends is a creative way to introduce your child to yoga. Here are some suggestions for how you can explore the book together:

- You may first wish to read the entire story together while you soak up the beat of each phrase and the beautiful illustrations. When you finish reading the story, go through each of the poses together.
- You may also enjoy doing the poses together as you read the book. As you read each page, stop and say to your child, "Let's see if we can become a _____ together."

- Read the description of a pose here in the note (rather than looking at the pictures) and see if your child can follow your verbal directions to move their body into the proper position.
- Strike a pose from the story and see if your child can name the pose.
- Turn to a random page and encourage your child to copy the illustration by matching it with the shape of their body.

No matter which method you choose to introduce this book to your child, follow the instructions in this Note (see "How to Do the Poses," below) to really get the most out of each of the poses.

### How to Do the Poses
Yoga is more than striking a playful pose. When you combine conscious, steady breath along with focused attention, you begin to balance the nervous system and develop the resilience to gracefully manage day-to-day challenges.

The following guide for each pose provides specific information for how to use your breath to flow in and out of each pose. Once your bones and muscles are aligned in the pose, see if you can hold the pose, but don't hold your breath. Take at least two long, deep, slow breaths through your nose with each pose. Counting the breaths together helps to focus the attention. You may discover that it is harder to slow down your breath with the more challenging balance poses. That's okay. Notice how it gets easier each time you practice. This is part of the fun of doing this together.

In all of the standing poses (mountain, chair, airplane, tree, and warrior) try to focus your eyes on one thing that is not moving. When you settle your gaze, your mind will settle as well.

After each pose, ask your child how the pose made them feel. Share how it made you feel. There is no right or wrong answer; the idea is to notice and be aware of your internal experience.

## MOUNTAIN

Stand with your legs slightly apart and feet flat on the floor. Feel how strong your legs are. Take a deep breath in, filling your belly and your heart with air. Imagine that this big breath fills you up so much that you grow another two inches taller. The top of your head can almost touch the sky. As you exhale, relax your shoulders, straighten your arms by your side, and turn your palms to face forward. Now imagine you are a big, tall mountain and take five deep breaths.

## CHAIR

Stand with your feet firmly on the ground and legs slightly apart. Take a big breath in as you reach your hands toward the sky. As you exhale, imagine there is a chair right behind you. Exhale as you squat down to sit. Your arms can stay straight, reaching above you, or you can bring your palms together and rest your thumbs on your chest. Can you hold your chair pose, breathing in and out five times? This pose makes your legs stronger so you may feel your muscles working hard to hold the pose. Focus your attention on your deep breaths. Does that make it a bit easier?

## AIRPLANE

In this pose it will be important for you to focus your gaze on something in front of you that is not moving. This will help your body stay balanced. Inhale and bring your arms out to the side, spreading your airplane wings from side to side. As you exhale, lean your body forward as one leg lifts behind you. This is the tail of your airplane. Can you keep your plane steady as you fly? Remember to keep your eyes focused in front of you and take your big, slow breaths.

Try it on the other side too. Is it easier to balance on one side more than the other?

## DOWNWARD DOG

To get into your downward dog, begin on your hands and knees. Make sure your front paws are spread wide as you push into the ground. Take a deep breath in and as you exhale, push your tail up to the sky, straightening your legs. You are now in an upside-down letter "V." Look up at your belly button, or through your legs. Try a different breath here. Take a big breath in through your nose. To exhale, open your mouth, and stick out your tongue. Maybe you even roar like a lion as you let all the air out. Try it a few times. How does that feel?

## TREE

Get ready for another balance pose. Focusing your eyes on something in front of you will help you to stay balanced. Begin with your feet together. Bring your palms together and your thumbs to rest on your chest. Slowly begin to peel one foot off of the floor. Bring that knee out to the side. Bring the bottom of your foot to rest on your calf. Your leg becomes a low branch. Your arms are your upper branches. Would you like to stretch them to the sky? Don't forget to breathe. Try that on the other side as well.

## WARRIOR II

Step your feet wide apart. Inhale your arms out to the side so they are the same height as your shoulders. Turn your right toes out to the side. Now bend that knee as much as you can, but keep your left leg straight. Do you feel your leg muscles stretching here? That's okay. What can you do to help your body relax in the pose? You guessed it—use your breath! On your last big breath in, straighten both legs as you reach your arms up to the sky. Now turn your warrior pose to the other side.

## CHILD'S

Come onto your hands and knees. Take a breath in through your nose. As you exhale, bring your bottom to rest on your heels. Bring your forehead to the floor and stretch your arms on the floor in front of you. This is a great pose to use when you are feeling overwhelmed. Stay here for a full minute to rest your head on the ground and feel the weight of your body over your legs.

## COBRA

This pose stretches the spine and opens the heart. It is fun to do facing each other like two snakes in the grass. Lay on your belly keeping your two legs together and stretched straight against the floor. Your forehead can rest on the floor as well. Place your hands under your shoulders. Take a big breath in and push your hands into the floor so that you can lift your snake head up through the tall grass. Exhale with a long, slow "hisssssssss." Breathe in through your nose and "hisssssssss" all the air out a few more times.

I hope you enjoy sharing and exploring yoga with your little one(s). Remember, these "child-friendly" poses are part of a regular "adult-friendly" yoga practice as well. The benefits of yoga are universal. As you playfully engage in this story together, allow yourself to feel, be present, and relax. You are your child's best model of how to *bee calm* in this world.

ALLISON MORGAN, MA, OTR, E-RYT, *is a pediatric occupational therapist, registered yoga teacher/trainer and the founder/director of Zensational Kids, an educational company teaching evidence-based practices of breath, movement, and mindfulness. She is a highly sought-after speaker who provides insight and inspiration to school communities who wish to address social-emotional learning and mental health care with an inside-out approach to building resilience. Visit zensationalkids.com.*

## About the Author

FRANK J. SILEO, PHD, is a New Jersey licensed psychologist and the founder and executive director of The Center for Psychological Enhancement in Ridgewood, New Jersey. He received his doctorate from Fordham University in New York City and is consistently recognized as one of New Jersey's top kids' doctors. He is the author of eight other award-winning children's books, including *Sally Sore Loser: A Story about Winning and Losing, Don't Put Yourself Down in Circus Town: A Story about Self-Confidence, A World of Pausabilities: An Exercise in Mindfulness, Did You Hear?: A Story about Gossip,* and *Bee Still: An Invitation to Meditation.* Dr. Sileo teaches mindfulness to his patients, and to schools and organizations. He enjoys doing Vinyasa yoga. Visit drfranksileo.com and @DrFrankSileo on Twitter.

## About the Illustrator

CLAIRE KEAY also illustrated *Bee Still: An Invitation to Meditation.* She works from her small studio at home illustrating children's books and stationery. Claire lives in the South of England. Visit clairekeay.co.uk, @claire_keay on Twitter, and @sherbet_lane on Instagram.

## About Magination Press

MAGINATION PRESS is an imprint of the American Psychological Association, the largest scientific and professional organization representing psychologists in the United States and the largest association of psychologists worldwide. Visit maginationpress.org.